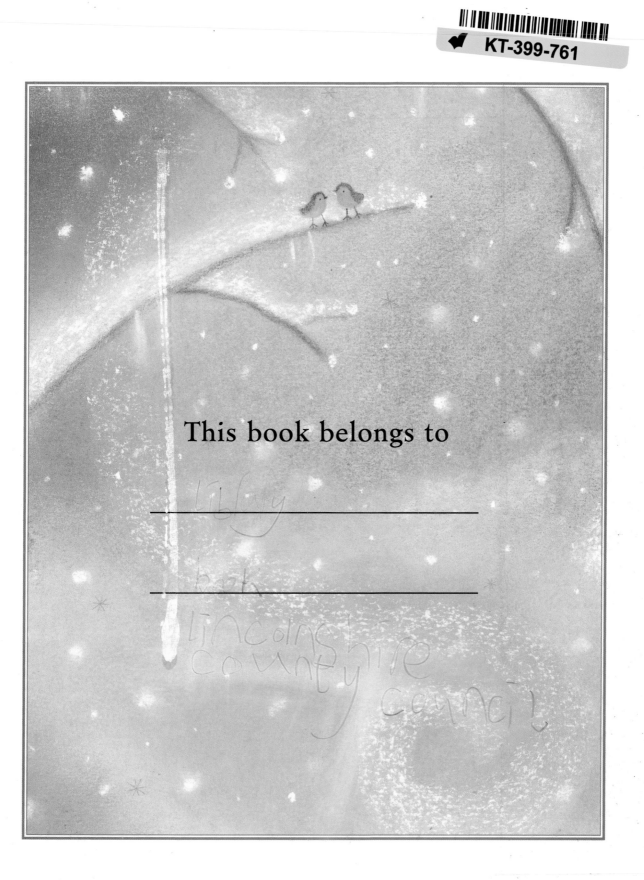

This book belongs to

Infny

book

lincolnshire
county
council

For Jacquie

C.F.

To all little children who love nature and animals such as bears,
the symbols of untouched and wild forests

D.K.

First published in Great Britain in 2007
This paperback edition published in 2008 by

Gullane Children's Books
185 Fleet Street, London, EC4A 2HS
www.gullanebooks.com

1   3   5   7   9   10   8   6   4   2

Text © Claire Freedman 2007
Illustrations © Dubravka Kolanovic 2007

The right of Claire Freedman and Dubravka Kolanovic to be identified
as the author and illustrator of this work has been asserted by them in accordance
with the Copyright, Designs and Patents Act, 1988.

A CIP record for this title is available from the British Library.

ISBN: 978-1-86233-727-5

Printed and bound in Indonesia

Little Bear's Special Friend

Claire Freedman • Dubravka Kolanovic

GULLANE
CHILDREN'S BOOKS

One morning Little Bear woke from his deep, winter-long sleep.

"Hurrah! It must be spring!" he cried excitedly.

Stretching and yawning, Little Bear peered out of his cave and blinked
in surprise. The woods were white with snow. Icicles hung from the trees.

"It's still winter!" gasped Little Bear. "I've woken up too soon!"

Little Bear burrowed down in his bed again, but he just couldn't sleep.

Little Bear's paws crunched deep
into the snow as he padded outside.
"Hello!" he shouted. "Is anyone awake?"
But the caves only echoed with deep rumbling
snores – his bear friends were still fast asleep.

Little Bear flopped down in the snow, feeling terribly lonely.
"I'll have no friends to play with until spring comes!" he said sadly.

"I'll be your friend!" called a voice.
Little Bear turned round in surprise. It was a little snowman!
"My name's Sparkly," laughed the snowman. "Cheer up, Little Bear.
Let me show you how much fun winter is!"

So Little Bear and Sparkly
skipped together through
the frosty woods,

and whizzed down
slippy-slidey snowdrifts.

They broke off icicles
to write their names
in the snow,

LITTLE BEAR   SPARKLY

and caught tickly
snowflakes on the
tips of their tongues.
"Winter is fun, Sparkly!"
Little Bear said. "I'd like
to wake up early every year!"

One day, as they played, Little Bear
slid into a tree and was showered with snow.
"Look out!" he called. "I'm the Big Bad Snowbear,
and I'm coming to get you!" And, giggling,
Little Bear chased Sparkly all through
the snowy woods.

"You're my best friend forever!" Little Bear
whispered to Sparkly one dark night. Snowflakes
glittered like falling stars in the bright, white moonlight.
"You're MY best friend forever!" Sparkly smiled.
And they hugged each other tight.

At last the snow stopped falling. Sparkly showed Little Bear the other animals living in the wood.

"Little Bear!" called Tuft-tail squirrel. "Help me dig up the acorns I buried last autumn!"

"Little Bear! Sparkly!" shouted Flinty Fox. "Let's go skating on the ice!"

Little Bear had great fun playing
with Tuft-tail and Flinty. But Sparkly
was his special friend.

Little by little the days grew warmer . . .

Then, one day, Sparkly told Little Bear,
"Spring will be here soon, and I must go away!"
"GO AWAY?" cried Little Bear, shocked. "Why?"
"Because Little Bears sleep through winter, and in the spring Snowmen
go away to where the snow never melts," Sparkly said gently. "That's how it is."

"But that means we'll never
see each other again!" said Little Bear.
"Best friends always find a way of
being together!" Sparkly promised.
"You'll see, Little Bear!"

Then Sparkly and Little Bear held
each other close for a long, long time.

There was a new sound in the woods.
The drip-drip of melting snow and ice. Little Bear
woke up one morning and rushed outside. The sun
shone and flowers blossomed everywhere!

"Hooray, spring!" shouted Little Bear excitedly
as he saw his bear friends had woken up at last.
"Sparkly, come quickly – it's spring!"
There was no reply.
Sparkly had already gone . . .

"Goodbye, Sparkly," Little Bear whispered sadly. "I'll miss you."
"We all will," agreed Tuft-tail and Flinty.

Little Bear cheered up as he played with his bear friends. But as spring came and went, he often thought about Sparkly.

When the bears climbed trees, to get sticky, yummy, honey, Little Bear laughed, "Sparkly would love this!"

As they splashed in the cool stream on hot summer days, he said, "Sparkly and I ice-skated here."

And whenever Little Bear met Tuft-tail or Flinty,
they remembered the fun times they'd shared.

Winter was on the way again. The bears filled their caves
with warm leaves, ready for their long winter sleep.
"See you next spring," they yawned.
"Sleep tight!" waved Little Bear.
"Don't let the bear-bugs bite!"

Soon he was fast asleep, too.
Little Bear slept . . . and slept . . .

. . . until he was stirred by someone's gentle nudging!
Little Bear opened his eyes.
"SPARKLY!"
"I woke you just a tiny bit early, Little Bear," Sparkly whispered.
"Best friends always find a way to be together!"
"They do!" cried Little Bear happily.

And, together, Little Bear and Sparkly skipped outside,
into the whirling, swirling, softly-falling snow.

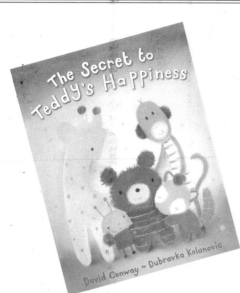

Another Dubrava Kolanovic book for you to enjoy . . .

The Secret to Teddy's Happiness
written by
David Conway

More from Gullane Children's Books

The Lamb-a-roo
written by
Diana Kimpton
illustrated by
Rosalind Beardshaw

Blame it on the Great Blue Panda!
written by
Claire Freedman
illustrated by
Emma Carlow &
Trevor Dickinson

Ferdie and the Falling Leaves
written by
Julia Rawlinson
illustrated by
Tiphanie Beeke